Mischief,
Mad Mary,
and Me

Mischief, Mad Mary, and Me

DAWN KNIGHT

Illustrations by Jared Taylor Williams

AN AVON CAMELOT BOOK

With special thanks to Nancy, Naomi, Father Mike, Dr. Midelfort, Mrs. Helen Trane, Robin Roy, Peggy King Anderson, Judy Bodmer, Katherine Bond, Janet Carey, Roberta Kehle, and Jan Keller.

AVON BOOKS, INC.
1350 Avenue of the Americas
New York, New York 10019

Copyright © 1997 by Dawn Knight
Interior illustrations by Jared Taylor Williams
Published by arrangement with Greenwillow Books, a division of William Morrow and Company, Inc.
Visit our website at **http://www.AvonBooks.com**
Library of Congress Catalog Card Number: 96-23212
ISBN: 0-380-73135-5
RL: 3.2

First Avon Camelot Printing: November 1998

Printed in the U.S.A.

OPM   10   9   8   7   6   5   4   3   2

FOR IAN, MY SON,
AND LANDREE, MY DAUGHTER,
AND *SEA*, WITH LOVE

Contents

1

The Hole in the Hedge

We crept along the hedge.

It was my dad's hedge, and it ran all the way around our yard. My dad never trimmed it so it grew up wild as a thicket. I used to think it would grow up into the sky like in "Jack and the Beanstalk," but it never did, of course. Spring was the only time the hedge was tame. In spring tiny white flowers tamed it, but it was winter now, and the hedge was bare and poky, and snowflakes fell right through it.

My best friend, Oly, was behind me. I turned around and walked backward. "Shhh!" I said.

"What?"

"Your boots are snapping." And they were. Oly had his brother's green boots on, and the toes snapped when he walked.

"Shhh yourself, Brit!" he said, and turned me back around.

My dad's hedge was as thick as any wall. It was so thick nobody could get through it, except for where there was a hole. The hole was by the sycamore tree in the backyard. All the kids in La Crescent (that's the apple capital of Minnesota, stuck down in the southern part of the state and close to the Mississippi River) cut through the hedge. My dad was really mad about it, but he couldn't stop them.

Peter, a kid in my class and the principal's son, lived on one side of the hedge. Our houses faced the street. Mad Mary lived right behind me.

She'd lived there forever. She was a hundred and fifty years old, kids said. She used to live in Alaska, and she'd been on the Iditarod. That's a sled dog race. All her dogs froze to death, kids said; that's why she moved here. She went to work for the parks department, and we saw her all the time, driving around in her red truck. Kids were always checking out what was in the back. Park stuff, Oly said, but Peter said he knew what she really used her truck for. He saw her dig up a grave once.

I'd talked to Mad Mary only twice. Once she told me my dad was looking for me, and once she

2

asked me if I wanted a ride and I said no. My dad said she was our neighbor, but I wouldn't call her that. She had a No Trespassing sign up. A real neighbor wouldn't put up a sign like that. That sign drew us kids the way the hedge did. We took to spying over there. She caught us and yelled, "Stay off my property, you hear?" That's when we started calling her Mad Mary. Word got around. We cleared off streets when she drove by in her red truck. We cleared out of stores when we saw her. But we didn't quit spying.

That's what Oly and I were up to now: spying. We crept up to the hole in the hedge. The snow was like a giant muffler, and it was quiet. Scary quiet.

"I'll go first," I said, and pulled the branches apart. The No Trespassing sign hung from a tree, rusty and lopsided, just like always. A wisp of smoke from Mad Mary's chimney drifted over the hedge.

There wasn't much else to see. Just snow and oak trees and Mad Mary's red truck. Spying wasn't as much fun in winter because she wasn't outside.

"It's my turn," Oly whispered.

It was boring while Oly looked. He always took

forever. He'd look and look, and when he was done, I'd ask him, "What did you see?" And he'd say, "Nothing." But this time Oly gasped.

"Let me see," I said.

Oly wouldn't budge. He was like my little sister when she hung on to my leg, a bug I couldn't shake off. I gave Oly a shove, but he stood solid. I squeezed in front of him while the hedge scratched me in the face. He tried to push me out of the way, but I held on.

Then we gave up shoving and looked through the hole in the hedge together. At a bear.

A bear? I couldn't get a good look at it because of the oak trees. But it was big and dark and in the middle of Mad Mary's yard.

Oly started blinking. Oly always blinked when he was scared. "You never told me Mad Mary kept bears."

"I didn't know," I said.

"But a *bear*? Can she do that? I mean, we live in a town."

"I guess so. Anyway, she is."

"Maybe it's Peter," Oly said. "He's got that bear costume, remember?"

"Maybe."

The bear rolled its head our way and disappeared behind the oak trees. We stared through the hole in the hedge, waiting for it to come back. Or for a look at Mad Mary. Or for something to happen.

And it did. The hole turned dark. I felt animal breath, and I heard a noise. It was low and wet, and it sounded like sniffing.

"The bear!" Oly shouted, and took off running with his scarf flying out behind him and snow blowing off his back.

I didn't run. It was the first time we'd seen something through the hole in the hedge all winter, and I wasn't going to miss it. The wind came up, raw and whistling through the hole. The bear rattled the branches. My knees gave out for a second, but I inched closer to the hole and looked through.

A great dark head stared right at me. I let go of the branches, and they whipped closed. My legs took me after Oly. But even as I was running, I knew I wouldn't forget that dark face I'd seen; I wouldn't forget it, not ever.

2

Underground

Oly didn't stick around. He ran past our snow-men to my underground house and threw the door open. That bear must have scared him good.

My house was a basement. It didn't have a house on top of it like the other houses on our block. The roof was about three feet off the ground. In summer the roof was so hot your feet burned when you walked on it, and in winter it grew icicles that hung over the windows. We had two doors, an outside door and an inside door. The outside door stuck up over the roof, making our house look like a hat.

We moved here when I was three. I can still remember the workers digging the hole for our underground house, the biggest hole I'd ever seen. My dad said we'd build a regular house on top of it someday, when we had the money.

Next to our house we had a garage. Oly thought it was funny that we had a house *under*ground and a garage *above*ground, but we had to have a garage or the car wouldn't start. Winter in Minnesota is that cold.

I dodged the snowmen, after Oly. All my life I'd come running into our house so fast I couldn't stop myself. The next thing I knew I'd fall down the stairs. There'd be a big crash. That was me, hitting the inside door. Today I stopped myself so that I wouldn't fall.

My dad stood at the bottom of the stairs, frowning at the trail of snow on the floor. He had on his old gray fishing hat, the one with the floppy brim. He wore it all the time, even in the house.

Oly's mittens hissed on a ledge at the bottom of our oil stove. I added mine. We exchanged secret looks. My sister, Bo, shuffled by in Mom's shoes. She had a bad cold, so she was still in pajamas.

My dad hung our coats above the stove. "How would you kids like some hot chocolate?"

"Sure," Oly said.

"With marshmallows," I added.

"I want one, too!" Bo said. She was three and wanted everything I had.

Oly kept looking over at me. I couldn't wait to talk to him about the bear. Alone. I knew he wanted to talk to me, too. We warmed our fronts and backs until the hot chocolate was ready.

My dad handed us two cups with a marshmallow swimming in each one. I took a sip. It helped slow down my heart. I'd heard of bears coming into people's houses and eating their supper. I hoped this one wouldn't—if it was a bear. I wasn't sure what it was. It was big and furry, but was it really a bear?

"Come on," I said, nodding. My closet was right under the stairs. I liked my closet because it had a door, the only door in our underground house.

"Pirate," Oly said, and went into the bathroom.

"Pirate" was the word we used when somebody had to go to the bathroom. Our bathroom didn't have a door, either. It had walls, though, made from bookcases. A pirate's chest was right next to it.

I glanced up at the window. That bear or whatever it was might follow us to school. We'd better watch out.

I put the hot chocolate on the floor and sat on

my bed. A folding screen made a wall between the living room and bedroom. My family had two beds, side by side. Bo and I slept in one, and my parents slept in the other.

Oly came out of the bathroom, and we went into my closet. My dad had painted my name, Brittany Bennett, on the door in big yellow letters. Oly fumbled for the string to the bare lightbulb and pulled it. My closet flooded with light. We sat on a blanket on the floor.

"That bear might be dangerous," Oly said. "Maybe we should call the police."

I took a big drink of hot chocolate. It burned going down. "It wasn't a bear," I said.

I'd been thinking about it when I was coming down the stairs and while my dad was making hot chocolate.

"Then what was it?" Oly said.

"A *dog*!"

I thought Oly might say, "Oh, my gosh!" or "What kind of dog?" or "That big?" but he didn't. I guess Oly didn't like dogs as much as I did. I knew every dog in La Crescent. I kept track of all the strays that came through our town, too. Oly said I was going to be a dogcatcher when I grew up, but that wasn't true, of course. I was going to be a veterinarian, specializing in dogs and cats.

Oly turned his flashlight on and put it under his chin. It made his eyes dark, and he looked like a ghost. "Naw, Brit," he said, "that thing was too big to be a dog."

"There are big dogs, Oly."

"It could be something else."

"Like what?"

"A werewolf."

"Oly, you're making that up!"

Oly leaned back into the shadows. "You never know with Mad Mary. And that thing was in her yard."

Oly was right about that. I started rocking on my legs the way I liked to do when we talked about Mad Mary. We always talked about her in my closet, and we always told the same stories about her. I knew what Oly was going to say, and he knew what I was going to say, but we liked doing it anyway.

"Remember what Peter did in second grade?" I said.

"Yeah!" Oly said. "Mad Mary caught him stealing watermelons off her porch."

"He took off like a rocket."

"But he was carrying four watermelons and they slowed him down."

I rolled up my jeans. They were wet. "It was just one watermelon, Oly."

"Mad Mary threw tomatoes at him, Peter said. Chased him all the way across town."

"It was just off her property, Oly," I said.

"We saw him up at the apple stand, remember? He had watermelon seeds and juice all over his T-shirt."

"Peter never liked watermelons much after that," I said.

Oly pulled his socks up, which meant we were at the end of the story. We both shivered. I grabbed two Indian blankets from my bookcase, and we wrapped up. My closet was nice, with all the blankets on the floor, a dog calendar on the wall, and a bookcase at one end. But it was cold. And it smelled musty.

My dad knocked on the door, opened it a crack, and slipped us a plate of doughnuts. My dad made his own doughnuts. He used to be a chef in a restaurant. I can still remember the big black pots and pans hanging from the ceiling and the freezer large enough to walk into. That was before my dad got sick. He has emphysema;

that's a lung disease. Mom doesn't want him to work anymore. She just wants him to stay home with me and Bo.

Oly drank the rest of his hot chocolate. We each bit into a doughnut. Bo banged on the door, but I ignored her.

"So what about that bear we saw?" Oly said.

"It was a dog."

"A bear."

"No, it was a dog!" Oly knew it was a dog, he just wasn't going to admit it, so I ignored him. "I'm going to go looking for it."

"Where?"

"At Mad Mary's. That's where we saw the dog, so that's where we should look first."

Oly shone his flashlight in my face. "Bear, you mean. What if that thing's hers?" Oly liked to think up problems.

"It's not," I said. "Mad Mary doesn't have a dog, unless she just got one. And if she just got one, wouldn't I see it or hear it barking?"

"You would, unless it's a bear."

"It's not, it's a *dog*! A stray."

Oly was being a chickenhead. He knew how much I wanted a dog. He said I'd get a dog when I grew up if I didn't get one before that, but we both thought that was too long to wait. We were always on the lookout for dogs. La Crescent didn't have a humane society or we would have gone there. We'd go to the library. Oly'd look at bird books, and I'd look at dog books. I couldn't decide which dog I wanted, if I had to pick. I liked every dog I saw. If that bear dog were mine, I'd take it everywhere. I'd bring it in my closet. I'd let it sleep on my bed.

I drew a dog on my jeans. "So are you coming with me?"

Oly's eyes were big in the shadowy light. I could tell he was thinking about it. Oly was thinking about it his way, and I was thinking about it my way. I wanted Oly to come. We'd been best friends ever since he'd moved here; that was in second grade. Since then lots of kids had moved here, but nobody like Oly. We were in the fourth grade now. My birthday was four months before Oly's, so I was older.

"You bet!" Oly said.

I jumped up. My stomach rolled over once, then twice. But I didn't know if we could find that dog in all the snow. And I wondered if it ever got cold.

3

No Trespassing

I heard the washing machine start up. It was right outside my closet, next to the hot-water heater.

"Brit—" my dad called.

I opened the door. My dad was pouring soap into the washing machine. He always said to let the soap and water mix before adding the clothes. He had an armful of Mom's work clothes. She was a nurse at a hospital.

"What?" I said.

"Go up and shovel off the roof."

"But, Dad! Oly and I have something important to do." More important than shoveling.

"Whatever it is can wait. The roof can't."

Our roof was flat. Snow piled on top of it, and

all that weight pushing down made the roof leak. My chore was to shovel it because I was the lightest one in our family, besides Bo, and she was too little.

"But, Dad! Can't I do it after supper?" We had a dog to track down.

"No, I need you to do it now, before we get any more leaks." We had four leaks in our roof, leaks that left brown rings on the ceiling. We used pots to catch the drips.

My dad looked up at the icicles outside the windows. I heard a wheeze in his chest from his emphysema. "Brit—"

"Okay, I'll shovel it." But I'd have to shovel fast or the bear dog might be gone.

Oly and I grabbed two more doughnuts and yanked our coats down from above the stove. Our mittens were warm. Bo started to pull on her boots, but my dad stopped her. We ran up the stairs.

Outside, the snow was really coming down. It hid our town, muffled everything, buried our house in white. Snow piled on top of snow, higher than our roof, and if it was a cold winter, it wouldn't melt until spring came.

The shovels were in the garage. We had plenty of shovels. Everybody did. "I'll do the windows," Oly said.

"Good. Then we'll be done faster." I was itching to find that dog.

I climbed on our roof and pushed the shovel, just stopping myself from running. If my dad caught me running on the roof, he'd be mad. I liked being up there. In summer when it rained, there was a lake on our roof. I'd stand in it and cool off my feet before I swept the water off.

I glanced over the hedge at Mad Mary's house. "We have to hurry, Oly."

Oly threw a shovelful of snow over his shoulder. "I'm hurrying."

A snowplow couldn't have gone much faster than we did. Fifteen minutes, and we were done. We put the shovels back in the garage and ran to the hole in the hedge.

The hedge rose up thick and wild, the way it always did. We hunkered down by the hole. Oly was as jumpy as a rabbit. My hands were sweaty inside my mittens.

"If you see Mad Mary, run," I whispered. "We'll meet up later."

Oly stuck his thumb up, and we pushed

through the hedge. Right off I saw Mad Mary's big stone house. Not at all friendly looking. It stood in the middle of oak trees, far back in the icy yard. Ivy hung over the corners of the windows, and without leaves the ivy looked like a lot of bony old arms. In summer bats were always crawling into the attic. We'd never seen them, but Mad Mary had. That's what she told my dad.

I scanned the yard. No bear dog. "Come on," I whispered.

We crept under the rattly brown leaves of the oaks and around to the backyard. There wasn't much back here. Drifts up to my waist over by the fence. A bat house. It was wood, and it had slits underneath for the bats to crawl in and out.

"The dog's not here," Oly whispered.

I glared at him. "We haven't even looked yet! Come on."

The snow came down, thick and fast enough to turn Oly's hat white. We crept across the backyard. I glanced up at the roof, wondering how the bats got in. My dad thought it was through the attic vents. Mad Mary told him they crawled under the closet door and flew around in her clothes. I wished that would happen to me.

Oly's coat was over his chin. "The dog's not

here," he mouthed. I should have been ready for that.

"The dog's not—"

"Shhh!" I shoved Oly in the shoulder, and we almost got into a fight right there, but we couldn't. Not in Mad Mary's yard.

"Let's go!" I whispered.

This time Oly went first. We crept quiet as cats around the corner of the house. Dog tracks! I thought they might be the bear dog's, but Oly shook his head. I knew what he was thinking; the tracks might be Sunflower's. She was the biggest dog in La Crescent, and she lived right around the corner.

Snow fell off a branch, and we jumped. We started to walk alongside the house; then we heard a noise like a window going up.

"Who's there?" someone said. My heart sped up. I glanced at Oly. His eyes were as big as eggs.

"Who's in my yard?"

The voice was sharp as a thistle. Oly didn't wait around. He took off at a run with his boots snapping and kicking up snow. I didn't run. I was the fastest runner in our school, but my feet wouldn't move. That was crazy, I knew, but I hadn't found that dog yet.

"Can't you kids read? That sign says No Trespassing!" Mad Mary leaned out an upstairs window. She saw me, clear as anything. A feeling colder than snow went up my legs. She threw her arm out, and snow mixed in her hair. She looked like somebody I'd never seen before, a person who lived way down the Mississippi somewhere or in a history book, somebody I forgot as soon as I closed the book.

"Don't they teach you reading in school?" she yelled.

My feet woke up, and I ran for the hedge. I was waiting to feel a tomato or something hit my back when a dark thing raced by. It was big and then *wham*! It hit me, and down I went. It yelped, and we rolled in the snow. Then it found its feet and leaped up.

I covered my mouth. The bear dog!

"Don't you kids come back unless you want something, you hear?" Mad Mary yelled.

That thistle voice. I jumped up; the dog was gone. I pushed through the hedge and came out in our yard. The smell of the hedge came with me on my coat. I didn't see Oly or that dog anywhere. Not anywhere.

4

Snowball Fight

I stood for a minute, letting my heart slow down and looking at the snow. It was still coming down. Already it'd raised our yard up an inch.

That dog was like the snow, I thought, soft and cold. I pressed my mittens to my face and smelled them, where I'd touched him. I wondered where he'd gone. I hoped he wouldn't leave La Crescent. If he did, he'd have to go down the highway, and he wouldn't like that; the cars came too fast. The only other way out was up the bluffs, but the snow was too deep up there, even for a bear dog.

I broke an icicle off the roof. He was a male, I'd seen that. Brown, not black, like I'd thought. I couldn't look for him anymore now; my dad would be mad if I didn't check in. But I'd start a dog watch, and tomorrow Oly and I would go on a dog hunt. I wasn't giving up until I found him.

I caught a snowflake on my tongue and went in. I didn't know where Oly was; he'd show up, though.

Inside, light came in the windows, bright from the snow. Our house wasn't near so bright in summer. It was cool and shady, like being under a tree.

"Oh, Brit's here," Mom said. She was home from work. She had a robe on, the way she always did. Grandma had sent it to her from Kentucky.

"You look cold," my dad said. "Better sit by the stove for a while."

We didn't have central heating; we just had an oil stove, but it threw out lots of heat and was good for warming mittens and boots and Bo's undershirts when she was sick. I took off my boots and socks. My feet were red. Bo was sitting in a wok on the kitchen floor in her cowboy boots. She came and sat on my foot and coughed. Her cold was worse, I could tell.

"You're gettin' sick," I said.

Bo shook her head. "Am not."

Right away I thought of pneumonia. Bo caught

21

it every winter, sometimes twice a winter. She couldn't fight off germs very well, Mom said. Bo wouldn't eat or drink anything, and she'd end up in the hospital. I don't know why she got sick so much when I never did. Peter once said she had AIDS, but she didn't; she just got sick a lot.

Mom opened her robe and wrapped it around Bo. "You need to be in bed, honey."

"But I like it out here," Bo said. She wanted to be by everybody.

"Okay, Brit will make you a bed on the couch, but we have to move it first." Mom pointed up. "There's a leak in the ceiling. See?"

I wrapped an Indian blanket around me. "So when did we get the new leak?"

"Just now," my dad said.

I didn't care at all about the new leak; neither did Bo. She liked to pretend she was a dog and drink out of the pots that caught the drips from our ceiling. I knew my dad cared, though. He looked up at the ceiling about a hundred times a day.

My dad pushed the couch against the long white wall. I carried end tables. Mom got the lamps. Bo stood in the middle of the floor in her cowboy boots. "I want Max," she said.

Max was my box turtle. He lived in an aquarium on top of the pirate's chest. "Okay," I said, "I'll get him."

I got a pillow, a blanket, Bo's blue teddy bear, and Max. I was coming back with my arms full and Max under my chin when I heard a noise at the window and looked up. Boots, going back and forth. Some kids were up there.

The first thing they did was peek in our window. I couldn't tell who it was because they had hats over their faces with holes for the eyes and mouth. One kid might be Peter, though. He was always looking in our windows. Once he almost caught me getting into the bathtub. I was still mad about it. I heard giggling. Then those kids climbed on our roof and ran right over our heads! The ceiling sagged and crackled.

My dad threw the door open and ran upstairs. His fishing hat blew off, he moved so fast. "Stay off the roof!" I heard him shout. "And keep off!"

My dad could shout forever, but it wouldn't do any good. Those kids were gone through the hedge on Peter's side. Right now they were probably tearing across his yard.

I dropped Max and Bo's stuff on the couch and pulled on my boots. I was sick of Peter and his friends running across our roof.

Outside, it was snowing so hard you couldn't see anybody, if somebody was there. "Peter!" I yelled. "I bet it's you!"

Somebody laughed on the other side of the hedge. I ran past my dad and through the frozen garden.

"Where's your coat?" he called, but there wasn't time to answer.

I elbowed through the hedge and came out in Peter's yard. Nobody there. I didn't know where Peter and his friends were. They could be running around the house or across the street in the schoolyard. There were lots of places to hide over there. I ran up to the corner of Peter's house and waited. My hands were red and stiff. Goose bumps broke out on my legs.

After a while I saw Peter and his friends slink back across the schoolyard with their hats in their pockets and their faces red as peaches. They glanced around, looking for me. I made a snowball. When they were close enough to the house so I could see their breath making smoke, I threw it.

Smack, it hit Peter square in the ear. He yelped like a puppy, then started to cry.

A shiver ran down my legs, mixing with the

goose bumps. I didn't mean to hit Peter there, and so hard. I stepped out from behind the house. He saw me, and his face twisted up. For a second he looked like a wolf.

"You live in a pneumonia hole!" he yelled.

"Pneumonia hole, pneumonia hole," his friends chanted.

I'd heard that before, because of Bo. I wasn't sorry anymore that I hit Peter. I whirled around. A snowball hit me on the back, but it didn't hurt. I elbowed through the hedge and ran back across the garden. There was Mad Mary's window, up above the other side of the hedge. We sure had great neighbors.

"Did you see who it was?" Mom asked when I came in.

"No, but I think it was Peter."

My dad put his fishing hat on. "If I ever catch—"

"We need a watchdog," I said.

"Yeah," Bo said from the couch.

Mom slipped her hands up the sleeves of her robe. "What we need is a new roof, Leslie. It can't wait much longer."

Leslie was my dad. He stared at the new leak awhile, then got the tray of tomato plants from the kitchen table and put them on top of the hot-water heater. He'd started them early for the garden.

My teeth were chattering. I wrapped an Indian blanket around me and sat on the back of the couch. Behind me the wall was damp. Bo held Max in the crook of her arm. "Why do you keep looking up at the windows?" she asked.

I didn't know I was doing it that much. "I'm looking for a dog," I whispered.

Bo sat up, and Max slid down her shirt. "What dog?"

"I call him Bear, but that's not his name," I said. "He just looks like a bear. Watch for him."

Bo looked up at the windows. I didn't say any more about that dog, but I knew Bo wouldn't forget. She'd look for him all the time now. That's how little kids are. Maybe I shouldn't have told her.

Outside, the icicles hung in uneven rows. Mom slipped a thermometer into Bo's mouth. I looked down at her little pale face, and I didn't know. Maybe she was going to get pneumonia again. She looked awfully sick.

5

Dog Hunt

On Saturday Oly and I sat in my closet. We were going back to Mad Mary's to look for that dog. We knew he was still hanging around; we'd seen his tracks in her yard and mine. I don't know how he came and went between our yards without my seeing him, but he did. I started calling him Houdini.

I turned my dog calendar back to March. Bo had it on July for the picture of the dalmatians. Oly turned his flashlight on and put it under his chin. I liked watching him do that. It was one of my favorite things he did.

"We better be more careful this time," I said.

"I know."

"Mad Mary caught us over there a few days ago. Who knows what she might do if she catches us again?"

"We know what she'd do," Oly said. "String us up by our boots."

I stuffed my hair down my sweatshirt, and we went out of my closet. We didn't trip over Bo's toys, the way we usually did. My dad had put them in the toy basket.

Bo was worse; her cold had moved into her chest. She might have pneumonia, Mom said. Mom had taken her to the doctor's, and we were waiting to find out.

Oly and I went into the kitchen. My dad stood on a chair, looking at the ceiling. Bread was rising on the counter. Folded laundry sat on the kitchen table.

"Did you fix the leak, Mr. Bennett?" Oly asked.

My dad touched the wet ceiling, as if he were testing bread. "Winter's a bad time to fix it, Oly."

"What about the slick seal?" I said. That was a sealant my dad put on the roof every summer. It ran into the cracks and crevices and smelled up our house, but it stopped the leaks for a while.

"I'm afraid the roof's just worn out, Brit. The sealant won't help anymore."

"You getting a new roof, Mr. Bennett?"

"We have to, Oly. The roof won't make it

28

through another winter." My dad squinted at the ceiling. "Your dad's going to help build it."

"Cool!"

I covered Oly's mouth so he wouldn't ask any more questions. He took the hint, and we left. On the way out I saw my dad put his hand on his knee and cough. His emphysema again. I ran back and gave him a handkerchief.

Outside, the sky was so blue and cold it was like a giant piece of ice. It made me cold just to look at it. My eyes watered, the snow was so white. Usually I didn't like winter. I didn't like wearing double pants and socks, an extra sweater, plus a coat, boots, mittens, and hat. They weighed me down. Then with all that weight on I'd go out and look up at the bluffs that stayed white for so long I'd forget they were ever green. But my dad said nothing was so beautiful as snow and that the bluffs were resting. If they didn't rest, spring couldn't come.

Winter wasn't bad today, though. We ran to the hole in the hedge. I bit my mittens and pulled them up. "Let's split up this time," I whispered. "We'll be harder to see."

Oly stuck his thumb up. "If you see Mad Mary, whistle."

We elbowed through the hedge. A few of the branches were broken from our going through. I didn't like that, but there was so much hedge. I guess it didn't hurt.

Oly went left, and I went right. Snow crunched under my boots so loud I thought Mad Mary might hear. I didn't see the bear dog, but I didn't expect to, either. Not this soon. The house looked as if it didn't want visitors. The curtains were closed. The door was in shadows. Oly and I never saw anything on her porch, not even a lawn chair in summer. Nobody ever visited at all, except the bats.

I headed behind the house, then stopped. There was something on her porch. It was small and white. I stared at it. A *soup bone*. Mad Mary had a soup bone on her porch. That seemed funny. I could see a carton of milk, or a block of salt for the deer that came down from the bluffs. But a soup bone?

Then it hit me. I glared at the house, daring Mad Mary to come out, and ran over to Oly. "I found a bone on her porch!" I said, not bothering to whisper.

I thought Oly might say, "Are you kidding me?" but he didn't. He was staring at the bat house.

I shook Oly's arm. "I found a bone, I said. Mad Mary's feeding that dog!" I thought Oly might say, "No way, she can't do that!" but no.

I kicked the snow, and it blew up in my face. I couldn't see Mad Mary with a dog. I couldn't see one on her porch or in the back of her truck. Why would she want a dog? For a second I tried to guess what her life was like, but I couldn't. Her husband was dead; I knew that. I saw him through the hedge once a long time ago. He was going into the house and there was a lot of green from the trees and he looked pale. He had cancer, Mom said. I shook my hand hard. Why was I even thinking about it? I never thought about Mad Mary at all before that dog came.

I dragged Oly over to the porch and pointed at the bone.

"Hey, Brit," he said, "that's somebody's foot!"

"Oly, it's a soup bone. I should know, my dad's a chef."

"She's got skeletons in her basement, I bet!"

I threw my arms out. "Forget the bone! Did you see the bear dog?"

Oly pulled his hat down so the blue stripe was over his eyes. "Nope," he said. "And hey, we better get out of here."

Oly's boots snapped as we ran across the white yard. I couldn't believe it. Mad Mary wanted that dog, the same as I did. The thought of Mad Mary and me wanting the same dog almost turned me into a snow-woman right there. What would I find the next time I came over: a doghouse?

I had to stop it. I backtracked, took the bone, and dropped it in my pocket. A window didn't go up; a door didn't open; a hand didn't reach out and grab me. Nothing happened, nothing at all. Oly didn't even see.

6

Ghost Dog

After that bone scare I knew we had to find the bear dog before Mad Mary did, so Oly and I started a dog hunt.

All the time, I held my hand out, pretending I had a dog on a leash. I didn't know where that dog was. We looked around the ice skating rink. It was full of kids going around in dizzy circles, and there was a mitten on the ice, but no dog. We looked under the highway. After that we went down to Skunk Hollow (that was Oly's favorite place in summer). We went looking around the grocery stores, too, in case that dog was hungry, but he wasn't there. I started calling him Ghost. He sure knew how to stay hidden. I guess he didn't know about me.

My chin was cold, and it scratched on the collar

of my coat. Oly's whole face was red. We went into Bauer's market to warm up.

Oly looked at bat houses. I wanted to get some dog biscuits, but they didn't have any so we went over to Quillin's grocery store. They had three kinds: milk, liver, and cheese. I smelled each box, trying to see which one a dog would like the most.

Someone came down the aisle, a tall woman in a scratchy-looking coat and no hat. I didn't know who she was at first. Then I saw a red truck through the window.

"Oly!" I tried to whisper, but it came out like a shout.

"What?"

"It's her!"

"Who?"

It was Mad Mary and nobody else. She walked toward us, quick. She had a bucket over her arm with an ice scraper sticking up and a bag of dog food. *Dog food!* I knew who that was for. My eyes skimmed over the bucket and stopped at her face. Her eyes were gray, like Bo's. I didn't like them being the same color as my little sister's. She had shoes on instead of boots. Nobody wore shoes instead of boots in Minnesota in winter. My dad said you could get frostbite and lose your toes

34

that way. But why was I even wondering about it? I didn't care.

She stepped toward us, quick. I felt a fight start up between us. "You kids stay out of my yard, you hear? You might get hurt. Now, I'm not telling you again."

I thought Oly should say something, but he didn't. He was hiccuping. Oly always hiccuped when he was scared. I couldn't say anything; I had her soup bone in my pocket. She might find that out.

Mad Mary's lips tightened, and she went on as if we didn't hear her. "There's footprints all over my yard."

Oh, yeah? I thought. What about dog tracks? They're all over your yard, too.

Nobody said good-bye. Oly pulled me down the aisle, and on the way I grabbed a box of dog biscuits. Cheese. If Mad Mary could feed that dog, I could, too. I paid for the biscuits, then threw her a look that said "You stay away from that dog." I don't know if she saw it.

Oly bought a bag of birdseed, and we ran down the block. We didn't stop until we reached the end of it. Our breaths made smoke in the frosty air.

"Did you see what Mad Mary bought?" I said.

"Yeah, dog food," Oly said. "They shouldn't have let her buy it."

That was crazy, I knew. Oly said things that were too crazy to be true but that made you feel good anyway. He was a great best friend. "I wonder where she'll put it," I said.

"In a bowl probably."

I kicked a chunk of snow. It spiraled over by Oly, and he gave it a kick. "I *know*. I mean, where?" Then I covered Oly's mouth. I knew where: right where the bear dog would find it.

When Oly wasn't looking, I dropped the soup bone in a snowbank. Nobody'd find it until spring. Oly tossed a handful of the birdseed he'd bought on the ice. "Are you ever getting a bird, Oly?" I asked.

"Nope, but I might get another cat, a white one."

Oly already had a cat; his name was Washington. I thought Oly should get another one, he liked cats so much. He shook snow off a little pine. Besides cats, Oly liked trees; he liked barn swallows, too, but they wouldn't be home until spring.

I threw a snowball at a tree. "Do you know what today is?"

"March twentieth."

"The first day of spring."

We looked all around. All the roofs had hats of snow, and the snowbanks came up to our shoulders. A car was buried in one. I was glad we didn't have to dig it out.

The sun was bright and cold. I wrapped my fingers around my thumbs to keep them warm. Then we did what we did every year when spring came on the calendar, but not to our town. We looked for signs of spring coming.

"See any icicles dripping?" I asked.

Oly looked around. "Nope."

"How about spring coats?"

Oly shook his head.

"Any oak leaves on the ground?" Some oaks hung on to their leaves all winter and didn't let them go until spring.

"A couple," Oly said.

"What about barn swallows?" I said; then I covered Oly's mouth again. I knew better than to ask. It was way too early for barn swallows. It wasn't until spring that you saw the little swallows flitting in rafters and sheds and in the barns around La Crescent. But they couldn't come home until there were insects. They had to have something to eat on the way here.

The box of dog biscuits rattled under my arm. We went back to our dog hunt, but we didn't find that dog. He didn't know I was looking for him, I guess.

Not one sign of the bear dog. Not even one sign of spring.

7

Watch Out for Turtles

When I got home, I sneaked across Mad Mary's icy yard far enough to see her porch. She had a bowl of dog food out. Just like I thought!

I elbowed back through the hedge and ripped my box of dog biscuits open. So what if Mad Mary was feeding that dog? It didn't mean anything. Anybody could. He wasn't hers. If she'd bought him, I would have seen him and heard him barking. He was a stray.

I dropped some biscuits in the snow by the sycamore tree. I put some in my pocket, too, in case I ran into the dog. La Crescent wasn't that big. I just might.

Inside our house my dad was sitting at the kitchen table with the seed catalogs for the garden. His eyes were dark under his fishing hat. Right away I knew something was wrong. He put an arm around me, held me tight. He didn't even wait for me to take my coat off.

"Bo has pneumonia," he said. "She had to go into the hospital."

That shouldn't have surprised me, but it did. It was like somebody'd jumped out from behind the folding screen at me in the dark. Suddenly we were missing two people, Mom and Bo. It changed our house. I'd have the bed to myself, and Bo wouldn't be kicking me under the table at breakfast. That sounded nice, but it wasn't.

My dad put his hand on my knee. "Your pants are wet. You better change, Brit. We're going to the hospital."

"But, Dad! I just saw Bo this morning."

My dad put his coat on. "That's different; Bo wasn't in the hospital this morning. She'll want to see her big sister."

Bo had Mom; she didn't need me. Besides, my dog biscuits were out. What if that dog came while I was gone? "I'm not going!"

My dad ignored that. He got Bo's crayons, checkers, Mom's sweater, and a book. I thought he'd yell, but he didn't. He didn't hurry either.

He took his time putting on his boots. "All right," he said slowly, and went upstairs.

I stood by the door, listening to the stairs creak. "Dad!" I shouted.

Silence, then: "What?"

"Wait!"

I ran back to the bedroom. Mom's cream rugs were on the floor in front of the beds. I wasn't supposed to step on them. I walked on them, looked back, and saw footprints. I wondered if anybody would notice. Not Mom; I didn't have a mother. She'd be at the hospital with Bo. Sometimes I thought she lived there.

My dad's tomato plants were still on top of the hot-water heater, leaning toward the window. I put dry pants on. Max watched me from his aquarium. Bo liked Max a lot; sometimes more than I did. I got a crazy idea. I picked Max up and hid him under my coat. My dad wouldn't even know.

Mom had the car, so we had to take the bus to the hospital. While we were waiting for it, Mad Mary drove up to the bus stop and talked to my dad.

It seemed that anywhere I was, she was. I held

Max under my coat and walked the other way. I thought they might be talking about me trespassing over there. My dad took forever. Finally he came and stood by me, his shoulders pushed up against the cold.

"I think she misses Alaska, Brit."

"Why?"

"She likes winter."

I sank my boot in a snowbank. "There's winter here, Dad."

"It lasts longer up north, honey."

I didn't see how anybody could like winter *that much*. The sun didn't get up until eleven o'clock in some places.

My dad didn't say anything else, so I guess they didn't talk about trespassing. I was glad about that. The bus came, and we got on. Max rode on my stomach, under my coat. My dad didn't even notice.

I looked out the window at the streaks of snow going by. We were on the Pike, the road to the Mississippi River. Backwater from the river was on one side of the road; Blue Lake was on the other. In summer water lilies grew up and turtles crawled out from the water and across the road. They did that to lay their eggs. We'd hear about them on the news. "Watch out for turtles on the road," the radio announcer would say, and Bo and I would look out the window to make sure the turtles got across the road okay. But there weren't any turtles out there now. Just snow and more snow.

The road climbed, and up ahead was the Mississippi. I liked this part, crossing the big river. The bus whined, and the girders of the bridge flashed in front of us. I looked down. There it was, the Mississippi. Ice ran up and down the sides, but the middle of the river was clear. I saw *water*. I hadn't seen water since last November. The ice was breaking up! Chunks of it floated down the middle of the river. I knew what that meant. Spring!

I pressed my face to the window. It was cold; I didn't care, though. In winter the Mississippi froze over, but even under the ice it raced along. Nothing could stop the Mississippi. Not even winter could freeze it and hold it still.

"You're like the Mississippi," Mom always said to me. She'd curl my hair around my ear and say it. She said it so much I believed her, but sometimes I felt like a piece of mud, too.

We came to a stoplight. The Mississippi was

behind us. Max slid off my stomach, and I put him back on.

"Bo won't be able to talk much," my dad said. "She's sick. You understand."

"I know, Dad. Bo's been sick before." I hated being told what I already knew. "Let's get her a balloon."

"Good idea," he said.

I heard a wheeze in my dad's chest from his emphysema. "You okay, Dad?"

"Fine," he said, but I could tell he couldn't breathe very well. A red truck drove by. I thought of Mad Mary and got mad at myself for even thinking of her. I felt in my pocket. The dog biscuits were still there.

We bought Bo a balloon, then took the elevator to her room on the third floor.

Bo was there, of course, in an elephant nightgown. I didn't like seeing her in a hospital bed; I was used to her in our bed at home. Her chest pushed in and out, as if it were work to breathe. She looked at me, but she didn't smile.

I tied the balloon on the end of Bo's bed. My dad started telling Mom about Mad Mary and how he was going to give her some tomato plants.

She didn't have a green thumb for tomatoes, she'd said. I knew that. I never saw any in her garden.

Grandma called, and we took turns talking to her. I held Max under my coat. His claws were right on my bare stomach! I had to get him off me.

Very carelessly, like, I took off my coat and put it on the bed. Then very easily I hid Max under it. I didn't want my parents to see. Max was just for Bo. I'd wait until my parents weren't looking; then I'd surprise her.

My dad read "Little Word, Little White Bird," a poem from the book he'd brought. He was always reading grown-up books to us. Bo's blue teddy bear fell on the floor. I picked it up, and she put my coat over it. She did that so it wouldn't get sick, I guess. That's what she did at home.

Everybody was listening to Carl Sandburg, the man who wrote the poem. That was okay, except Max's nose poked out of my coat. I yanked it over him.

"Don't," Bo said, and pulled my coat her way. I put my arm down on it. Nobody saw. I made a face at Bo and pointed at Max, but she didn't see.

Mom looked up, and I stopped. "Why don't you

45

get a root beer?" she said. She thought that would give me something to do.

"I don't want one."

"I thought you loved root beer," my dad said.

I licked my lips. "I do, but—"

Now Max's foot was out. I inched my coat over him. "Don't," Bo said.

My dad eyed me and picked up my coat. I put my arms down on it. What else could I do? We got into a tug-of-war. I'd never been in a tug-of-war with my dad before.

"Brittany Bennett!" he said. He didn't believe I was doing this. "Stop it—or else!"

I knew what that meant. I let go and covered my face. Through my fingers I saw Max!

Suddenly this wasn't so funny. I was going to be kicked out of Bo's room. I'd have to go sit in the lobby all night. I mean, this was a hospital. There were a lot of sick people in here. Max had germs. What if he went to the bathroom on Bo's bed?

"How on earth—" Mom said.

"I thought I smelled something," my dad said.

Mom and Dad looked at me, eyes blazing. Then Bo pushed herself up on her elbows and giggled. A big giggle, loud enough to crack the ice on the

Mississippi, and my parents started to laugh. Bo leaned over the bed. Ruffles from her nightgown went across her chin. "Did you find Bear?" she whispered.

The bear dog. It took me a second to find Bo's ear; her hair was all messy and sticky. "No," I whispered, "but I'm looking—" I dug in my pocket, took out a dog biscuit, and showed it to her. We traded smiles.

I wrapped Max in my sweatshirt. Next time I'd bring the bear dog up here. But I had to find him first.

8

Dog Watch

Mom stayed at the hospital with Bo while my dad drove us home. On the way he talked about the garden. He was going to have two this year, one for vine plants and one for plants that grew up and down like carrots. I didn't listen much, but I liked his voice filling up the car. It was too dark to see the Mississippi. Max rode on my stomach, under my coat.

While my dad put the car away, I ran to the sycamore tree. I had to find out if the bear dog had found my biscuits yet. Mad Mary's yard light was on, shining over the hedge. I knelt in the snow; I felt the cold go through my jeans.

The dog biscuits were gone! I couldn't find them anywhere. I jumped up. Max almost fell out, but I caught him. That dog had come! I shook the sycamore tree until the branches danced in the dark sky.

Bear would be back, and he'd be hungry. I dug the biscuits out of my pocket and dropped them in the snow. Then I stood still, listening. All I heard was my dad. "Brit," he called, "time to come in."

Inside our house I took off my boots while my dad emptied the pots that caught the drips from our ceiling. Those never-ending leaks! We couldn't be gone too long or the pots got too full.

"You must be hungry," he said.

I looked up at the windows. It was hard to keep my heart still with that dog around. "Starved."

"Good. I'm making pizza."

While I put Max back in his aquarium, my dad ran oil into our stove. I sat on my foot and drew dogs, and when I looked up, I saw a pool of oil on the floor. My dad had forgotten about it. He'd let the oil run over.

"Dad!" I yelled, jumped up, and turned the oil off. My dad came around the stove, put his hands on his knees, and swore. I put my arm around him. "It's okay, Dad," I said, but I knew it wasn't. Oil running over wasted money.

We got rags and mopped it up. When the pizza

was ready, we sat down to eat. I could still smell the oil. I caught strings of hot cheese on my tongue. Something scratched on the roof, and I looked up. "What's that, Dad?"

"I don't know, Brit. Kids don't run on the roof at night, not in winter. It could be a wild animal."

We'd had animals on our roof before. "A raccoon?"

My dad stood up. "Too small."

The sound went from one end of the roof to the other. Too light for a bobcat, too heavy for a fox. My hands started to shake. I jumped up, knocking my chair against the table.

"Brit—"

I pulled on my boots and ran upstairs. I switched on the yard light. It lit up the snow, threw shadows on the roof. A dog trotted out of the shadows. He was big, dark, furry. My heart beat hard. My dad came through the door after me. I didn't want him here right now.

"Get off the roof!" he shouted.

It was hard even to talk to my dad. "Don't yell at him."

"Whose dog is that?"

"Nobody's. He's a stray. I can get him off, Dad."

My dad frowned. "I don't know, Brit. Is he friendly?"

"Look at his tail." It was wagging. The dog's sweet, cold smell came across the roof to me. "Let me get him off, please, Dad!"

My dad's face went soft, and I knew he was giving in. He went downstairs and got my coat and mittens and handed them to me. "Stay in the yard," I heard him say. "It's dark out."

I nodded. When I looked at the door, my dad was gone. Alone. Alone with that dog. I smiled and put my coat on, my hood up, and walked along the roof. The dog kept his eye on me. He must be wondering what I was like. Was I a friend? Could he trust me?

"Come on, Bear. You need to get off the roof."

He swung his tail over his back. He knew what I wanted him to do; he just didn't want to do it. I couldn't climb on the roof; I wasn't allowed to, except to shovel it. I made a snowball, tossed it over the dog's head. He tore across the roof after it and jumped off. Graceful, for such a big dog.

I wanted to run, but I made myself walk around the corner of the house. I didn't need to run; he was right there across the roof. I came up nearer, careful not to scare him. The hedge was close, dark, warm. The only sounds were his breathing and Peter, in his house, playing the violin.

"Did you find those dog biscuits?" I said.

The dog pricked his ears. Mine was a new voice, I could tell. One he wasn't used to.

"I bought cheese. Thought you'd like that."

He swung his tail over his back. There was snow on his nose, ice on his chest. I wanted to check his paws for ice; I knew that could hurt a dog, but I knew he wouldn't let me. He needed time to get used to me, to my voice and my smell.

"You sure are big. I should call you Bear," I said, and laughed.

He nosed through the snow in the garden. It was deep there, up to his chest. I think he liked snow. If he liked snow, maybe I'd start liking winter. Then I couldn't wait; I had to pet him. "Here, boy," I said, patting my leg. "Come."

The dog stretched out his front legs, wanting to play. I held out my hand. He dashed up to me, caught my mitten on his teeth, and pulled it off.

"Hey!" I said. "That's mine!"

That dog wasn't listening. He shook his head and trotted under the yard light with my mitten. He looked beautiful in his scruffy coat. A door slammed over at Mad Mary's. The dog stopped and pricked his ears, and a cold feeling went through my heart. He remembered the dog food she had on her porch. He took off along the hedge, and I lost him. Then I saw him again out in the street. He disappeared into the schoolyard.

Gone again. Why was it that every time I found him, I lost him? My hand was cold. I stuffed it up my jacket sleeve, but it didn't help.

9

Mischief

In the morning, while we were having breakfast, the bear dog came to the window. I looked up, and he was there. He knocked an icicle off the roof before I knew it was true.

"Dad!" I said.

My dad glanced up from his waffle. "Looks like the dog's back. He must like it here."

"He does. He likes me!" I took a breath. "Dad—can I keep him?"

My dad opened the seed catalog and paged through it without stopping to look at any of the flowers or vegetables. I knew better than to talk to him while he was thinking, so I watched the dog knock another icicle off. The window was almost bare now. My dad finished his waffle; then he put his fork down.

"We have to talk to Mom, of course," he said, "but I think you can go ahead and put up some signs. Ask around La Crescent. Let's see if we can find out if anyone owns the dog first."

I hugged my dad; then I hugged him again.

"But I'm not promising anything, Brit," he reminded me. "We might not have room for such a big dog. He'll cost a lot to feed. There's the shots, the vet bills."

"I know, Dad." Any way I could keep him was okay.

I grabbed my coat, some waffles, and ran upstairs. The dog was in the garden, biting snow. He wagged his tail when he saw me. I fed him the waffles.

"Bear—" I said, petting his soft ears. I didn't know what to call him. I didn't like his old names—Bear, Ghost, and Houdini—anymore. I could call him Mitten because of that mitten he stole. Or Mitten Thief. But he wasn't a real thief; he was just playing. Mitten Mischief would be better or . . . just Mischief.

Mischief. I liked that! It was like humming, the way the sound stayed on my lips. I knelt in the snow. It was soft, and my jeans got wet, but I didn't care, I never got sick. I hugged him, then kissed him on the mouth.

"Mischief! How do you like your new name?"

He licked my cheek. I guess he liked it.

The sun came up, hitting the garage roof. Mischief followed me over to Oly's. We found him in the garage, sorting through nails with Washington, his cat. Mischief ran up to Oly, and he jumped back. I could tell he still thought Mischief was a bear.

"Is that him, the bear dog?" Oly said.

I felt a smile come on. "Like him?"

"Yeah, he's as big as a horse!"

I shook Oly until his hat fell off, I was so happy.

Oly gave me an old dog collar he'd found, and we put it on Mischief. I got a rope out of my garage, and we went to work making signs. I wanted to make them small so no one could read them, but that wouldn't be fair. Washington got paint on his whiskers. Oly had to wipe it off.

The signs said:

FOUND
One large, furry, brown dog.
Is he yours? If so call
Brittany Bennett at 555-2781
or
Oly Erickson at 555-9006

We taped the first sign on a tree by school. Mad Mary drove by in her red truck, and I looked the other way. "She stared right at us," Oly said.

I put a sign under my arm. "She caught us trespassing over there, that's why."

"She's got dog food on her porch."

"I know. I saw it. I won't let Mischief go over there." He still liked going back and forth between our yards.

I went back to taping the sign. Mischief put a paw on my bike. I don't know if he knew how close he was to being my dog. Very close. I didn't dare think about it too much, though. I didn't want to stop a miracle from coming, though I thought it picked a funny time to come, with Bo in the hospital.

"Think your dad's gonna let you keep him?" Oly asked.

I smiled. I think Oly knew what that meant.

We biked around La Crescent, looking for more places for signs. My pedal clinked as it circled. Mischief bit at my jeans, and it took me three blocks to get him to stop it. We left one sign by the apple stand and one by the hardware store.

Mischief ran through the slushy snow. On the way back Oly and I saw some icicles dripping. I knew what that meant. Tonight they'd freeze again, but I didn't care. Freeze, thaw. Freeze, thaw. That's the way spring comes to Minnesota.

At home I made a bed for Mischief out of a dryer box I'd bought from Peter. I wrote Mischief's name on it with a blue marker and put it in the garage. My dad let me bring him in my closet. I tried to teach him to "sit," but he wouldn't. Then I tried to brush him, but he kept biting the brush. He wasn't very good at minding.

Later the phone rang. I let it ring and ring ten times before I answered it. It was Oly.

"Don't scare me!" I said. "I thought you were somebody calling about Mischief."

"Hey Brit," he said, "have you got any glue?"

"Lots," I said. "Did you get any calls about Mischief?"

"Nope."

I hit myself on the chest. "Oh, good!"

The next day we biked around with Mischief, counting all the snowmen that were left. I kicked snow out of shady spots so it would melt faster. We dropped our bikes and hid from Mischief in Amy's garage. He went tearing past. Then he put on his brakes and came back and barked at us.

"Quiet!" Oly said.

He shouldn't have said that. Mischief planted two muddy paws right on Oly's chest.

"Down!" I said, but Mischief wasn't listening. I put my arms around his middle and walked backward, laughing.

"Crazy dog!" Oly said.

My signs had been up for a week now, and no calls. Brown spots of earth appeared in our garden. I decided brown was my favorite color. My dad said that was an odd favorite color for a young girl to have, but not me. I liked it. Mischief was brown, so was the earth, and I hadn't seen it all winter.

On spring break I ran into Amy, Chris, and Hillary, some kids from my school. Peter was there, too. His face had lost that wolf expression, so I guess he was ready to be friends again. I was, too.

"Is he your dog?" he asked.

"No, he's a stray," I said, "but I might keep him."

"Cool!"

"I love his fur," Amy said. "He looks just like chocolate."

"He has a cute pink mouth," Hillary added.

Mischief walked all around Hillary, sniffing her legs. "I think he smells your cat," I said.

"Or my pants. I had pizza for lunch and I dropped it."

Everybody laughed. I looked up at the blue-and-white sky. A kite dipped, climbed, circled. I didn't have to wonder anymore whether spring was coming or not. Spring was here.

The earth drank up almost all the snow, but there was still some in the bluffs, so Oly and I took a sled up. Oly said you could see the whole world from up there, and I wouldn't have thought so, but today I did. The air tasted like spring. It smelled like it, too, and that smell was on every kid's coat in school. Bo had never been up in the bluffs with us. Oly and I decided to take her this summer. We'd been to the hospital to see her. She was eating soup and crackers. My dad spent the night with her so Mom could come home.

Mischief stood on my foot, a thing he liked to do. His tongue dripped on a warm rock. We spotted Oly's house and La Crescent-Hokah Elementary School. My house was too small to see. I didn't look at Mad Mary's because of Mischief. But he didn't go over there much. Even with his rope off he didn't go over there, and it felt as if the hedge grew up between Mad Mary and me, thick and tall like in "Jack and the Beanstalk." It went back to the way it was before Mischief came. I didn't talk to her. I didn't see her. Peter said she moved back to Alaska. I thought I'd never have to worry about dog food on her porch again.

Then one day I saw her.

10

Spy Trip

Oly and I were on our bikes with Mischief, cutting across the school playground. It was full of murky brown lakes, the kind you see only in spring.

"Hey, Brit," Oly said, "look at that!"

I glanced up. There was Mad Mary driving by in her red truck. So she hadn't moved, like Peter said. I knew better than to believe Peter. Mud was all over the front of the truck, and something big stuck up out of the back. It had a tarp over it.

Oly waved his arm at me. "Come on!"

Oly didn't ask if I felt like spying. I didn't. The only reason I'd gone over to Mad Mary's this winter was to look for Mischief. I had Mischief now. But Oly was my best friend. He'd gone on lots of dog hunts with me; it was my turn to do what he wanted to do. That's what best friends did.

We biked home, and I locked Mischief in the garage. He barked like crazy, but I wasn't taking him, not over to Mad Mary's.

I met Oly at the hole in the hedge. "I'll go first," he said, stuffing homework up his jacket sleeve.

"Okay," I said, though I didn't want to. We pushed through the hedge.

The house surprised me; it looked worse with the snow gone. It looked older; the stones were darker and grayer. Mad Mary had put a screen door on. I didn't remember that from last summer. The dog bowl was gone. I looked up and down the porch, but it wasn't there. I shook my jacket sleeves down over my hands. I didn't like being over here. It reminded me of Mischief.

Oak leaves rattled and rolled across the yard. Oly sneaked up to the truck with me behind him. Mischief barked, and a shiver went down my back. If he kept that up, Mad Mary might hear him and come out.

We hunkered down on the other side of the truck, away from the house. Oly lifted up the tarp. "There's a lot of junk in here. Empty paint cans and cardboard and stuff." He rattled things around. "I bet she's taking this stuff to the dump!"

I let the air out of my chest. "Is that all?"

"A tree's in here."

That didn't sound very interesting to me, but it was to Oly. He crawled partway under the tarp. I waited. The wet smell of spring came on the air, and for a second I thought of winter—how the sharp, cold air goes in your lungs and makes them cold and what a funny feeling that is—but it was gone now.

"It looks dead," Oly said. His voice came out muffled.

"Okay," I said. "Let's go."

"The tree's coming with us."

"Oly, it can't!" He backed out muddy boots first, and I pulled him down. We crouched by the back tire.

"She's just gonna throw it away," he whispered.

"We should ask anyway."

"You know that flag in my room? I found that in a box somebody threw out."

"That's different. This is in her truck."

Oly wasn't listening. He dragged the tree out; it screeched on the metal bed of the truck. It was a little oak, and it still had most of its roots. "It

64

might not be dead," he whispered. "Maybe we can save it. Remember where this tree was?"

"Where?" I said.

"Over by where the fence meets the hedge in the backyard."

Oly remembered things nobody else could. That was one of the things I liked about Oly, but not now. "She'll know it's gone," I whispered back.

"So?" Oly said, like I was the crazy one here. Maybe I wasn't a spy anymore.

Oly rubbed the tree with his jacket sleeve. "Come on, we're taking it!"

We stood up, and I felt the light of day on me like a spotlight. We lifted the tree up and ran through the leaves, dragging the tree between us. Water from the grass splashed on my shoes. Oly dived into the hedge, and we pulled the tree through.

"Hold on!" I thought I heard somebody yell. "Hold on there!" But it wasn't Mad Mary. It was a voice in my head.

11

Mad Mary's Red Truck

Oly kept the tree in a bucket of water in his garage. A week went by, and by that time we knew the tree was dead for sure. Oly didn't want to take it back. We dragged it into his backyard.

Nobody called about Mischief, saying he was their dog. I didn't think anybody would call anymore, not in a town the size of La Crescent. My signs had been up for three weeks. Everybody had seen them fifty times each by now.

A sign was falling down by the apple stand, my dad said. I had to bike up there with Mischief and tape it back up. Mischief pushed through my legs, and dog hair came off on me. A lady in a purple coat saw us and smiled. I think she thought he was my dog.

We took the long way home, looking for barn swallows. It wouldn't be spring, Oly said, until the swallows came home. To me it wouldn't be spring until Mischief was my dog. But my dad hadn't said I could keep him yet.

I biked over the top of a hill, and Mischief barked. There was Mad Mary's red truck! It was parked on the side of the road, next to a stretch of crabgrass. The hood was up.

I whipped my bike around so fast the tires bounced. I wasn't going that way, not with Mischief. Besides, her tree was still in Oly's backyard.

"Mischief," I called, but he ignored me. He ran down the hill and jumped in the back of Mad Mary's truck.

"Mischief! Get out of there!" I flew down the hill on my bike. I never thought he'd do something like that, but Mischief was always mixing me up with Mad Mary. He used to hang out over there, that's why. She'd yelled at me twice now because I went in her yard to get him. This was going to be the third time she'd yell. I should have locked him in the garage.

My tire hit the back bumper of the truck. Mad Mary stepped out from in front of the hood and my stomach rolled over. She walked toward me quick and straight and put a hand on Mischief's snout. "Better get Dog out, girl."

"That's what I was going to do," I said.

I stood up on my pedals and grabbed Mischief. That part was easy. Then I pulled him over, nails scraping, and made him jump out. That part was hard. "I'm sorry," I said. I had to say something.

Her eyes fixed on me. We were up on a hill, and there weren't any houses around. I thought of how Peter said she dug up graves and Oly said she had skeletons in her basement. I didn't believe it, but—

"Somebody took a tree out of the back of my truck. You know anything about that?"

My stomach blew up like a balloon. She might talk to my dad or, worse, what if she called the police?

"Well, girl?"

I gripped the handlebars. I might steal, but I didn't lie. "It was me and Oly. I told him not to."

"Thought so."

I licked my lips. "I better go," I said.

She put a hand on my bike. "You better stay here. I'm gonna need help with this truck."

She walked quick toward the engine. I could

run, I had my bike, but Mischief might not follow me. "Girl," she said. "You coming?"

I rolled my bike down to where she was and got off. I stood next to her, but as far away as I could. I could smell her and her clothes. The smell was musty, like my closet.

She leaned under the hood. "It's the fan belt." I knew where that was; I fixed the car once with my dad. She got a stick and wedged it in the engine. "Here, pull on this. It'll hold the alternator tight."

I didn't want to, but I took the stick. The smell of grease came up from the engine. I watched Mad Mary's hands. They were black from oil and wide like an iron, and she had big knuckles. I'd never paid attention to what my own hands looked like until I had to draw them once in school. I found out I had long fingers and small knuckles.

"Somebody took a bone off my porch. Either that was Dog or that was you, girl," she said.

So she knew about that, too. "It was me."

"You give that bone to Dog?"

"No, I threw it in a snowbank . . . do you want it back?" That was crazy, I knew. I'd never be able to find it.

Mad Mary leaned back and laughed. "Well, girl, I sure don't need a bone. I ain't got a dog."

I knew why she didn't have a dog. It was because of me. She didn't say anything else; she just worked on the truck. Mischief stuck his nose between us and sniffed. I was still mad at him. Finally she took the stick out, held out an arm to make me step back, and slammed the hood. "All right, we're done." Then she stood, wiping her hands on a towel. "You tell your friend Oly to put the tree back, all right?" she said.

"You're not gonna throw it away?"

"That's right. It'll make good firewood."

I got on my bike. Mischief chased his tail, and Mad Mary smiled at him and wrinkles ran up into her eyes. For a second she didn't seem so crazy. She didn't seem so mad. She just seemed like an old woman.

"How's your sister?" she asked.

"Better."

12

Good-bye, Snowmen

I couldn't tell Oly about the dead tree. There wasn't time. We had to bring Bo home from the hospital. There wasn't any pneumonia left in her chest at all.

I helped carry Bo's stuff down our stairs. She got a dinosaur from Oly, crayons from Peter, and a box of toys from Grandma. Our shoes made a lot of noise going down. I didn't know how much I'd gotten used to just me and my dad until now.

Bo sat on the couch and bit off her mittens. "Mommy, can you make the snow go away?"

"It's almost gone, honey," Mom said.

"No, it's not." Bo kicked off her boots. "There's snowmen in our yard."

"They'll melt, Bo," my dad said.

"The sun will make them go away," Mom said.

Bo's face scrunched up. "But I want them to go away. Now!"

Why was Bo making such a fuss over snowmen? You never know what gets into a little sister. I knelt on the couch. "I can make the snowmen go away."

Bo wiped her cheeks. "You can?"

"Just wait."

I ran up the stairs, let Mischief out of the garage, and ran around the house. My dad held Bo up to the window. "Bear!" she shouted.

"No, *Mischief*!" I hadn't filled Bo in on his new name yet.

There wasn't much left of the snowmen. I took out their carrot noses and threw them in the garden. Then I stomped on them. I stomped and stomped, Mischief pawed at the snow, and Bo watched and clapped her hands.

Winter was over, over. And my little sister was back. And who knew? Maybe someday winter would come and Bo wouldn't get pneumonia. Mom said she'd outgrow it. We just had to wait.

My dad made spaghetti for supper and rhubarb pie for dessert, to celebrate Bo's coming home.

Mischief was muddy, so he had to stay outside.

He went from window to window while I helped Bo put the pictures she drew in the hospital up on the refrigerator. My dad cooked spaghetti sauce and read to us from *Siddhartha*. You could hear it everywhere in our house. I'd never heard it before, but sometimes I felt like I was there in India, in those words. I could almost feel the sun on me.

We sat down to eat. Bo sat across from me; that way if her milk spilled, it would hit my parents first. Mom smiled every time I looked at her. My dad had his good shirt on. I thought it was the right time to ask.

I took a breath. "Dad, can I keep Mischief?"

My dad looked up from the bread he was cutting. "How long have the signs been up?"

"Three weeks."

"And you didn't get any calls about Mischief?"

"The only calls I got were from Oly, asking for glue."

"Where did you find him, again?" Mom asked, pouring Bo's milk.

I hadn't told my parents that. I was afraid to. I didn't like the sound of what was coming. "Over at Mary's."

"Did you ask her?" Mom said.

I'd just talked to her. "No, why should I? She must have seen the signs. She didn't call or anything."

Mom kissed my arm, below my shoulder. "Ask. Maybe Mary knows who Mischief belongs to."

"But, *Mom!*" I gripped the table. I felt like shaking it until everybody's milk spilled, but I didn't. I didn't want to ask Mad Mary; I knew what she might say. The window above the stove went dark. Mischief. He'd made me so miserable, and so happy.

"Just ask," my dad said.

I put my elbows on the table. "If she says no, can I keep Mischief?"

I could see the yes in my parents' faces even before they said anything. "We'll give it a try," my dad said. "But you'll have to mow a lot of lawns and shovel a lot of driveways to help pay for his keep."

That should have made me happy, but it didn't. My dad gave me a piece of rhubarb pie, but I couldn't eat any. Not until I talked to Mad Mary.

13

Mischief, Mad Mary, and Me

I got the tree out of Oly's garage and dragged it through the hole in the hedge. Oly was supposed to bring it back, but he couldn't. He wasn't home. That should have made me mad, but I was too worried about Mischief.

Then I led Mischief through, keeping the branches away from his face. I leaned the tree against the back of Mad Mary's truck. I could have put it in, but I didn't. Why should I? I knew what she was going to say about Mischief. "Thanks for bringing him back. He's my dog. Good-bye."

I went up to her house and knocked. Before I was ready, before I knew what to say, she came. She didn't look surprised to see me. "Girl," she said through the screen.

What I'd been thinking made a hard ball in my stomach. "I brought the tree back."

She leaned into the screen so her elbow made a dent. "I see that." There were brown spots on her face, from being old.

When I didn't move, she said, "Is that what you came to tell me, girl?"

"No." I felt my stomach push up, making it hard to breathe. "Mom was wondering if you know who Mischief belongs to."

"Now why was your mom wondering that?"

"Because . . . he might be my dog . . . I mean, I might keep him . . . if you don't."

"Well, that depends on how you look at it," she said. She stepped out and stood on the porch. She had on an old sweatshirt with bleach marks. Her feet were bare, I saw. "Mischief—is that what you call him?" she said.

I nodded.

"Suits him. I called him Dog."

That's not a very good name, I thought. Mischief sniffed Mad Mary's jeans, but she didn't pet him the way I did. "He came around this past winter, looking for food," she said. "I let him in. Found out he liked kibbles. He liked the fire, too, so I covered a chair and let him lay."

I knew what was coming. Why didn't she just say it? "You think Mischief belongs to you, don't you?"

"Now what makes you say that?"

"Because you do."

"Dog found me before he found you, that's all."

I rubbed Mischief's chest. I felt a fight start up in me. "He was a stray. Anybody could feed him."

"I was the first one to do it, girl."

"But you didn't even give him a name!" I said.

"Dog, that's a name."

"Not a real one like *Mischief*!"

"I suspect you're right." Mad Mary bent over, picked up a clump of Mischief's fur, and let it go. "This is a winter dog. He won't like the hot weather. He'd like it in Alaska, though."

"You can't take him there!"

She fixed her eye on me. "Dog ain't moving. But it would only be fair, wouldn't it? After all the trespassing you did."

I wasn't a spy anymore, but she didn't know that. I thought of Peter—how he ran across our roof and peeked in our windows, how I didn't like it. "I'm sorry," I said.

"All right, girl."

Mad Mary sat on the porch. She told me to sit,

too, so I sat at the other end, by the railing. I watched her rub her feet. That reminded me of Grandma. It seemed funny to sit on Mad Mary's porch the way I sat on Grandma's. I wondered if any kids from school saw me and if they were wondering why I was sitting here instead of spying, but at Grandma's the kids would never wonder that. They'd know she was my grandma.

Mischief sniffed leaves in the yard. The oaks were letting them go, and soon there'd be too many to rake up, almost. It would take all the kids in La Crescent. Mischief came and stood with his paws on the bottom step. He licked Mad Mary's jeans. I couldn't stop him.

Something came up from my stomach. It tasted bad. I started to cry. Why did Mischief have to like her so much? Why did I have to find him over here? I was sorry I ever saw him through the hole in the hedge. I was sorry he'd come here.

"So what about Mischief?" I said.

She squinted at me. "You named him, girl."

I wiped my face. "So what do you want me to do?"

"Well, I don't know. I think you should say."

But I couldn't say; why did she want me to? I couldn't stay here either. I couldn't take Mischief, and I couldn't leave him. I didn't think, I just grabbed the rope and ran with Mischief to the hole in the hedge.

"Come back," I thought she'd yell, but she didn't.

14

The New Roof

I shut Mischief in the garage; I couldn't be around him right now. Then I had to get past Oly's dad waving and Amy calling me and down the road to where the houses thinned out and the bluffs rose up. Then I felt something at my side.

Mischief. Did somebody let him out? Did he get out? Maybe I didn't shut the door tight enough. He came up to me, dragging the rope behind him. It had been through a puddle.

I stepped back. Any closer wouldn't hurt too much. "Mischief, you shouldn't be here." He picked the rope up; it hung out the side of his mouth. His tail wagged once. "Okay, you might as well come."

My stomach felt queasy. We climbed up into the apple orchard. There was still snow in the woods around Stony Point. Wet grass soaked my jeans. I hung on to a tree so I wouldn't throw up.

Mischief wouldn't leave me alone. He nosed my hand, wanting to be petted. He didn't understand. I knelt in the grass, rubbed his furry head. "You're a good dog, Mischief. A good dog." I put my arms around his middle.

Soon as I could breathe okay, I stood up. "Come on, Mischief, let's walk."

We started across the bluff, between the apple trees. I can't remember the first time I came up here, but it must have been when I was little because I remember being afraid to do it. I was afraid I wouldn't be able to make it up to the top; that was Stony Point. Then I was afraid I wouldn't be able to make it back down. And that cave Peter said was full of rattlesnakes, the one he was always trying to get me into, I was afraid of that, too. I felt like that now. I had to decide whose dog Mischief was, and I was afraid. Only it was worse because there wasn't any place like Stony Point to climb to. The place was inside me.

I looked down. So much water was on one side of our town: the Mississippi, backwater from the river, and Blue Lake. The highway was there, too. The bluffs, where I was, were on the other side. In spring the apple trees bloomed, and the bluffs turned white and pink, and my dad looked up at them every time he got out of the car, and I looked up, too, when I swept water off our roof.

In the fall La Crescent had an apple festival. We had as many hot dogs as you could eat and as much cider as you could drink. There was a parade, too. Everybody went, even Mad Mary. If I didn't see her all summer, I'd see her there. And if Mischief were my dog, I knew what he'd do: He'd run up to her and wag his tail. I think Mischief knew he was her dog before he was mine. It would be too hard, Mischief always telling me, reminding me whose dog he was. I wouldn't like it.

"Come on, Mischief," I said. "We have to go."

We headed downhill. My feet hit the clumps of dry, dead grass. The rope dragged behind us.

I tied Mischief to Mad Mary's porch, closed my ears to his barking, and started home.

"Girl!" she called, her voice pulling me back from the hedge. I looked up at the window. "Wait a minute. I'm coming down," she said. The window slammed shut.

I stood there stiff in her yard, but Mischief was

whining bad, so I went back to the porch. Mischief licked between my fingers. I'd been gone only two seconds, and he missed me, but not as much as I missed him. I wiped my face.

Mad Mary opened the screen door and stepped out. "I've been thinking about this dog, Brit."

"What?"

She knelt by Mischief. "Dog likes to roam, go from place to place. Some dogs are that way. You can keep a dog so it's safe, or you can let it go and fear it'll starve. I'd like us to keep this dog if he'll stay."

Us—keep him, keep Mischief? I wasn't sure what she meant.

"Dog would like it in your basement. It'll be cooler down there." She pulled up Mischief's fur and let it go. "Just too hot in Minnesota in the summer."

I opened my mouth, stared. "He could stretch out on the floor where there aren't any rugs and be cool."

"The coolest dog in La Crescent." A corner of her mouth went up in a smile.

Keep Mischief—both of us together? "But . . . where's he going to sleep . . . who's going to feed him?"

"Dog'll figure some of it out. The rest we'll have to, won't we?" She stood up, brushed wrinkles out of her clothes. "He's a big dog, so he'll eat a lot. I'll help with the food and vet bills. Talk to your dad, see what he has to say. Some folks share a lease on a horse together by trading the horse off every other day."

"I wouldn't want to do it that way," I said.

"Well, we don't have to."

I didn't know if I wanted to share Mischief at all. I'd always wanted my own dog. But that was before Mischief came. Now I didn't have a choice because I wanted Mischief more than any dog in the world. But I never thought I'd get him this way.

Mischief pushed my arm up with his nose. "I've got a dog bowl," I said.

"There's one over here, too."

"There's a bed in my garage."

"And Dog can sleep on my porch. Like I said, he's a roamer. He'll do some of the deciding." She opened the screen door. Mischief tried to get in, but I held him back.

"You handle that dog well, Brit."

I looked up at her.

"Dog'll be coming over; maybe you'll be coming, too, for a visit."

"Okay," I whispered.

I watched her bare feet as she went in. She knew a lot about dogs; she used to have all those sled dogs. Mischief stuck his cold nose through my arm. I kissed it. I opened my arm and kissed his mouth and the side of his face. He was my dog now, and Mary's.

I walked with Mischief to the hole in the hedge. It seemed funny to walk instead of run. When you walked, the hedge looked the same on this side as it did on the other side.

My dad stood with his fishing hat on, looking at the roof. I didn't tell him about Mischief. The idea of sharing him was new inside me, too new to even talk about. And who knew? I might like it. Sometimes you start to like something you didn't used to.

I looked at the roof. It rippled all the way across and sagged in the middle. Winter had been hard on it. "Are we ever getting a new roof, Dad?" I said.

My dad rubbed my hair. "This summer. Can you wait that long, Brit?"

I nodded. By summer the hedge would bloom again, tiny white flowers that looked like snowflakes, all the wild tamed out of it. At least for a while. The turtles would crawl across the road to lay their eggs again, over by the Mississippi. By then I would have talked to Oly. I would have told him Mary wasn't so crazy. But Oly might not believe me. He might have to find that out for himself, the way I did.

I patted my legs, Mischief jumped up, and I caught his paws. We did a little dance, Mischief and me. Then I threw a stick for him, next to our underground house. I chased him and chased him, but Mischief wouldn't give the stick back. But Mary and I would train him. It would take the two of us to do it, too.

That's the kind of dog Mischief was.